PETE JOHNSON

PIRATE BROTHER

Illustrated by Mike Gordon

PUFFIN

PUFFIN BOOKS

Published by the Penguin Group
Penguin Books Ltd, 80 Strand, London WC2R 0RL, England
Penguin Group (USA), Inc., 375 Hudson Street, New York, New York 10014, USA
Penguin Books Australia Ltd, 250 Camberwell Road, Camberwell, Victoria 3124, Australia
Penguin Books Canada Ltd, 10 Alcorn Avenue, Toronto, Ontario, Canada M4V 3B2
Penguin Books India (P) Ltd, 11 Community Centre, Panchsheel Park, New Delhi – 110 017, India
Penguin Group (NZ), cnr Airborne and Rosedale Roads, Albany, Auckland 1310, New Zealand
Penguin Books (South Africa) (Pty) Ltd, 24 Sturdee Avenue, Rosebank 2196, South Africa

Penguin Books Ltd, Registered Offices: 80 Strand, London WC2R 0RL, England

www.penguin.com

First published in Puffin Books 2002
Published in this edition 2004
This edition has been produced exclusively for Nestlé breakfast cereals

1

Text copyright © Pete Johnson, 2002
Illustrations copyright © Mike Gordon, 2002
All rights reserved

British Library Cataloguing in Publication Data
A CIP catalogue record for this book is available from the British Library

ISBN 0–141–31896–1

1. My Top Story

One day I found a cape at the very top of a tree. The cape was dark blue, with bright gold stars around the sides. And it was magic.

It made wishes come true.

I only found this out when I accidentally turned my younger brother, Harry, into a bluebottle. Reema, my best friend, and I had an awful job trying to

turn him back again, I can tell you.

Oh yes, in case you didn't know, my name is Jamie.

Here's something else you might not know. The most magic part of my cape is just inside the collar. That's where you'll find the number seven, all worked in gold. When you make a wish, you hold on to this part. Also, you have to water the cape before you make a wish. Don't ask me why. But the magic works only when the cape is wet.

Lately, though, the magic hasn't been working at all. I've made so many wishes and not one of them has come true. Is all the cape's magic used up? I don't think so. And I'll tell you why.

Sometimes, when I'm making a wish, the seven on the cape really sparkles. It dazzles my eyes. And I feel this funny tingling in my hands.

So that proves there's still a little magic in my cape, doesn't it? And it's trying so hard to get out and make my wishes come true. But it can't. If only I could help it. But I don't know what do. It's very, very frustrating.

I've cheered myself up by reading books about spells and magic. And there's

one book I've read over and over. It's
called *Brave Bill, the Magic Pirate*. Maybe
you've seen it. It's my all-time top story.

It's Reema's too. And Harry says it's his
favourite as well. But then he would,
wouldn't he? (He copies me in everything,
you know – it's so annoying.)

Anyway, *Brave Bill* is the story of the
youngest pirate ever. In fact, he was only

4

eight when he ran away to sea. He'd been living in this children's home which he hated.

His grandad left him a ship in his will. Brave Bill's grandad had been a pirate once, but he'd lost all his treasure. In fact, he'd lost everything except his pirate ship. And he wanted Brave Bill – his only living relative – to have it.

So one night Brave Bill crept away with some other children from the home. They set off to find his grandad's ship. Then he set sail on it, with the other children acting as his crew. They had lots of adventures and discovered masses of treasure. They buried this on their secret island, which no one else knew about. This was where they lived too, when they weren't being pirates.

Brave Bill wears a patch over his left

eye. And if ever you annoy him, watch out. Because then he will whip off his eyepatch and stare at you with his magic left eye.

The moment this happens you start to shrink. The longer he looks at you, the smaller you become. Once Brave Bill shrank someone down to the size of a peanut. But he doesn't do that very often. Only when he's really angry.

Imagine having Brave Bill as my friend! Oh, that'd be totally brilliant. No one would ever dare pick on me again. Not with Brave Bill close by. He'd always protect me. And knowing he was my mate would make me braver too. I could do things I'd never dreamt of – like being a pirate.

How I'd love to jump into Brave Bill's book and have some adventures with him. I've wished for that on my cape so often. But it's never happened.

On Friday at school though, we can dress up as our favourite character. Guess who I'm going to be?

On Thursday afternoon I tried on my costume. First I put on my old stripy pyjama bottoms. Next came a white T-shirt which had a red skull and crossbones sewn on to it by my mum. Then Aunt Nora found a grey jacket with gold buttons and gold braid around the collar and wrists. I was really pleased to have that. Aunt Nora also bought me a gold earring.

Lastly came two very important things: Brave Bill's eyepatch. I made that. And Brave Bill also wears a dead-smart hat. It's green and black and curled up at the front, and it has feathers on it. I made that too and it took me ages and ages.

When I'd finished I went and stared at myself in the mirror. Someone started laughing straight away.

Who else but Harry.

'You don't look anything like Brave Bill,' he sneered. 'Ha, ha.'

'Just shut it,' I snarled, 'or I'll fight you.'

This made him laugh even louder. Harry is two years and three months younger than me and he's half a head taller. I only come up to the middle of his ear. Talk about embarrassing. Actually, I'm one of the smallest boys in my class. And my nickname is – I'll just whisper it to you – 'the Shrimp'.

Harry ran off, still giggling about me trying to be Brave Bill. I changed out of my costume. And then the doorbell rang. Twice. That sounded urgent.

Harry and I rushed to the door. But Aunt Nora got there first. She's looking after Harry and me while Mum and Dad are in Scotland.

She's actually my mum's aunt, so she's like an antique aunty.

She opened the door. 'Oh, hello, Reema.'

'Hello, Aunt Nora,' Reema gasped. She was out of breath. 'Is Jamie there?'

'Yes he is – I mean, yes I am,' I replied.

'Well, I'll leave you two to have a nice little chat,' Aunt Nora said, going back to the kitchen.

'I've just had an idea about you know what,' Reema whispered. Then she saw Harry hovering about. 'But it's a secret.'

2. Reema's Brilliant Idea

Reema and I raced up to my room.

'So what's your idea?' I asked. I was getting excited already myself.

'Just wait a sec, though,' I said. 'I'd better check no one's listening outside.'

But to my great surprise there was no sign of Harry.

'Still, we should whisper,' I said.

Reema nodded, then hissed, 'You always make your wishes on the cape during the day, don't you?'

'Yes,' I agreed.

'How about trying a wish at night, and especially . . . at the witching hour.'

'Whatever's that?'

She smiled. 'I've just found out about it. I heard them talking on the radio. They were saying midnight is the witching hour.'

'Midnight!' I cried.

'Yes, they said that's when magic is at its strongest. So I was thinking, if you made a wish on your cape when there's

11

all that magic in
the air . . .'

'Some of it might creep into my cape
and help make my wish come true,' I
interrupted. 'Reema, that's really clever.'

'Oh, it was nothing,' she said, but she
looked very pleased.

'So tonight,' I cried excitedly, 'I'll set my alarm for five to twelve, wet my cape, hold on to the letter seven and wish. Can you guess what I'll wish for?'

Reema smiled. 'To step into the pages of your *Brave Bill* book. Oh, it'll be so brilliant if your wish comes true.'

'This time I really think it will,' I said. 'So why don't I wish for you to come too?'

Her eyes lit up. 'But could the magic stretch to two people?'

'I don't see why not. I'll give it a try anyway. So you'll be up and dressed at midnight, and ready to shoot off, won't you?'

'Oh, I'll be ready,' she cried eagerly.

Then we both stopped. We could hear something outside, a creaking noise. And we'd forgotten to whisper. In fact, we'd been shouting at the top of our voices. If Harry was outside, he'd have heard every word.

But when I opened the door there was no sign of him. That was a relief. You see, Harry doesn't know the cape is magic. But he's wondered about it. He even said, 'Your cape looks as if it could do spells.' Of course I just laughed.

That night I was so excited I couldn't get to sleep for ages. At last my eyes grew heavy and I floated off into a dream about Brave Bill.

Ring, ring, ring, ring. I jumped up in bed and switched my alarm off. It was five to twelve.

I got dressed as quickly as I could – after all, you can't go and be a pirate in pyjamas, can you?

Far away I heard the church clock

striking midnight. The witching hour had begun. Now the air was crammed with magic.

I went over to get my cape. At night I always put it over the chair at the bottom of my bed. Only it wasn't there. I hurriedly searched around my room. No sign of it. And something else was missing too. My *Brave Bill* book.

Harry.

I raced into his room. My cape was on his bed. So was my *Brave Bill* book. But Harry wasn't there.

He was floating above me in the air.

3. Harry Flies Away

I gave a little gasp of shock, then I cried, 'Harry! You ear-wigged on Reema and me.'

'Of course I did,' he laughed. 'It's the only way you ever find out things. And why didn't you tell me your cape was magic?'

'I didn't tell you,' I spluttered, 'because you spoil everything. Now, get down here at once.'

I jumped up to try and pull him down. But at that very moment he floated up even higher. He was touching the ceiling now.

'I always wondered what it felt like to be a bubble,' he grinned. 'This is such good fun. So, have you got a message for Brave Bill?'

'What?'

'I wished that I could spend the day on his ship,' Harry said.

'You have to copy me, don't you?'

Harry's body gave a little twist. 'Can't chat any longer, got to fly. Think of me on Brave Bill's ship, won't you, Jamie?'

And after saying that, he vanished. Then I noticed Harry had left a note by his bed. Here's what it said:

Dear Jamie,

I'm off to be a pirate with Brave Bill. I'll be home for my tea tomorrow. Tell Aunt Nora I'd like baked beans and sausages.

Bye for now,

Harry

P.S. I thought Aunt Nora might worry about me. So I wished that whenever she heard the words 'Brave Bill' she would immediately start smiling.

P.P.S. Don't be cross that I'm going to be a pirate instead of you.

Don't be cross! I was so angry I was shaking. I paced furiously around Harry's bedroom. It was my cape. Mine. Yet Harry was the one, off having brilliant adventures. It was totally unfair.

And what about poor Reema, waiting in her bedroom to be whooshed away. She was going to be so disappointed.

But had Harry used up all the cape's magic? Maybe there was still a little left for Reema and me. I picked it up. It was still wet. Then I pressed down really hard on the seven and wished. 'Number Seven, can Reema and me be with Brave Bill, please?'

I wished so hard. And the seven glittered and shone. I knew it was really trying to make my wish come true. My hands began to tingle. And then I saw this tiny spark, like the end of a firework.

The magic was starting.

So I waited . . . and waited . . . and

absolutely nothing else happened.

I thumped my way back to my bedroom.
I angrily flung on my pjgamas. Then I sat
up in bed, leafing through the pages of my
Brave Bill book. When I got to the last
page, I blinked in astonishment.

There was the usual picture of Brave Bill and all his shipmates. But now a new face had joined them. Guess who? Yes, that's right. My brother. I couldn't believe it. But there he was, laughing with all the other pirates.

Next morning when I woke up, the sun was streaming through my curtains. But I felt cross and grumpy. Then I sniffed. What was that awful pong? It smelt like old seaweed and smelly socks. But there was a salty tang to it as well.

I held my nose. Phew. My bedroom stank.

But what could be causing it?

I gazed around – and then I got the biggest shock of my life.

Someone was asleep on my chair.

4. Brave Bill Has Breakfast and a Bath

I jumped out of bed.

The stranger was a boy. A boy who had a patch over one eye and who was wearing a most magnificent pirate hat with blue, red and purple feathers sticking out of it.

It was Brave Bill! Here in my bedroom! The room started to spin round, just as if

I were on a ship during a storm at sea.

I tip-toed over to him. No, it wasn't a dream. He was really here. He was sleeping with one hand over his eyepatch.

And then Brave Bill's eye sprang open: it was the deepest, darkest blue you've ever seen.

'Ahoy, landlubber,' he cried.

'Ahoy, Brave Bill,' I quavered. 'I'm sorry if I woke you up.'

'I wasn't asleep,' he replied. 'I was only resting my eye.'

23

He jumped to his feet. To my surprise, he was exactly the same height as me.

He looked around. 'Not a bad little cabin.'

'Thank you.' Then I shook my head and cried, 'I just can't believe you're here.'

'Why ever not? You wished for me on that cape hanging over your chair, didn't you?'

'Well, not exactly.'

He frowned. 'What do you mean?'

'I wanted to join you on your pirate ship. That was my real wish. Only my annoying little brother got in first.'

'Oh yes, I remember him,' Brave Bill said. 'He just popped up out of nowhere.'

'So by the time I made my wish, Harry had used up practically all the magic. And there wasn't enough left to take me to your ship. But as you're magic anyway . . .'

'The cape was able to bring me to you instead,' interrupted Brave Bill. 'So, one moment there I was dancing the pirates' hornpipe, and the next I was being whooshed here.'

'I hope it wasn't too inconvenient for you,' I said politely.

'Oh no.' Brave Bill waved a hand dismissively. 'I felt like a change of air.

The journey took a long time, though. Lots of hold-ups.'

'The cape's usually very quick. But I guess it's working on reduced magic right now.'

Then I chanced to glance down at my *Brave Bill* book, which was still open at the last page. I let out a whistle of surprise. My brother was still there. But Brave Bill had vanished from the picture. There was just a silhouette where he had been before.

'Look at that,' I cried.

But Brave Bill just shrugged his shoulders. 'Well, I can't be in two places at once, can I?'

'I suppose not.'

'What's your name, landlubber?' he asked.

'Jamie.'

'Pleased to meet you.' He stretched out a hand. There were big, fat rings on every finger. And some fingers even had two rings on them. 'We're going to have fun today,' he laughed.

And it was brilliant to see him. I just wished he didn't whiff so much. The smell was making me feel quite sick.

Brave Bill decided to inspect my

bedroom. He strutted about, peering at everything. He even opened my wardrobe. Then he stepped back in surprise. He'd just spotted my pirate costume, all ready for school today.

I explained. 'At school we can dress up as our favourite character. So I . . . I'm dressing up as you.'

'Good choice,' he replied.

All at once we heard a voice calling from Harry's bedroom. 'Harry, Harry, where are you?'

'That's Aunt Nora,' I said. 'I'd better go and explain what's happened. I won't be long.' Then I had a thought. 'By the way, can any other people see you apart from me?'

'Of course they can,' Brave Bill said indignantly. 'I am a magic pirate, you know.'

I tore off to see Aunt Nora, the *Brave Bill* book under my arm.

'Hi, Aunt Nora,' I said. 'Lovely day, isn't it?'

She looked at me anxiously. 'I can't seem to find Harry.'

'Oh, don't worry about him. He's just gone off on a pirate ship for the day.'

'What!' she shrieked. Then I remembered what Harry had written in his note.

'He's with Brave Bill,' I said.

At once Aunt Nora's face broke into a big smile. 'Oh, that's all right.' Then she became puzzled. 'But who is Brave Bill?' As soon as she said his name she was smiling again.

'Look, there he is.' I showed her the cover of my *Brave Bill* book. 'And look, there's Harry.'

Aunt Nora gazed at the picture for a long time. 'Well, I suppose it'll be a nice change for Harry. And the sea air will be good for him.' Then she sniffed. 'Whatever is that awful smell?'

'We've got a guest, Aunt Nora. Brave Bill.'

Aunt Nora was grinning again.

'He's just popped out of his story and popped in here. Would you like to say hello to him?'

'Oh yes,' she said eagerly. 'Where is he?'

'Right here,' said Brave Bill, standing in the doorway. He bowed to Aunt Nora. 'At your service, ma'am.'

'Oh my goodness,' Aunt Nora cried. She took her glasses off, wiped them and put them on again. 'I've never had a pirate visit me before,' she exclaimed. Then she took a deep breath. 'Now, er,

Brave Bill.' Her lips immediately began twitching. 'I understand my nephew is spending the day on your boat.'

'Ship,' corrected Brave Bill.

'Yes. Well, will he be safe there? He is rather young to be a pirate, even for a day, you know.'

'Have no fear, ma'am. Brave Bill's shipmates will look after him very well.'

Aunt Nora looked relieved. Then she smiled at Brave Bill. 'Jamie's friends are always welcome to drop in . . . And I expect you'd like some breakfast.'

'I certainly would,' said Brave Bill. 'I've had nothing but stale bread and mincemeat for seventy pages.'

'So how would bacon, egg, fried tomatoes and toast suit you?'

Brave Bill smacked his lips appreciatively. 'Perfect.'

'Would you mind doing something for me first?' asked Aunt Nora.

'Name it,' Brave Bill replied.

'Go and have a bath, please.'

Brave Bill looked shocked. 'But there's no need, I had one last Christmas.'

'Well, if you don't mind me saying so, I think it's time you had another one.'

'Another one!' Brave Bill exclaimed. 'Great, shivering seaweed.'

'I'll make it two eggs,' Aunt Nora said temptingly.

Brave Bill looked at her, smacking his lips again. 'It's a deal.'

'Now, the bathroom is . . .' Aunt Nora began.

'I'll find it,' Brave Bill said, marching off.

'Aunt Nora, do you think Brave Bill could come to school with me today?' I asked.

'I should think so, dear.'

'But I'll only tell Reema who he really is,' I said.

'Yes,' Aunt Nora agreed. 'We'll tell everyone else he's your friend William, from far away . . . and he's dressing up today as well.'

Then I went back into my bedroom and put on my Brave Bill costume while the real Brave Bill was splashing about and singing sea shanties in the bathroom. It was all so exciting.

A much cleaner and sweeter-smelling Brave Bill came rushing downstairs. Breakfast was waiting for him. He scoffed it down eagerly. 'This is delicious,' he said.

'Would you like seconds?' Aunt Nora wanted to know.

'And thirds,' he cried. 'I wish I could

take some of this food back for my shipmates.'

'Well, perhaps I can make a few sandwiches for them,' Aunt Nora replied. 'How many of them are there?'

'Forty-three,' Brave Bill said.

'Ah.' Aunt Nora's voice fell away. 'Well, I'll see what I can do. Now,' she beamed at him, 'it's all arranged, Brave Bill. You can go to school with Jamie.'

'School.' Brave Bill spat out the word.

'I've told the school you're William, a friend of Jamie's. You will behave yourself, dear, won't you?'

Brave Bill grinned. 'I always behave myself.'

5. Brave Bill Becomes
Very Angry

Aunt Nora insisted on seeing me across
the road to school even though Brave Bill
was with me. But he didn't seem to mind.
Instead, he sniffed the air appreciatively.
'Strong breeze, bright sun, no clouds: a
perfect day.'

I was really happy too. But there was
something I had to tell him.

35

'Brave Bill, although I'm dressed up as you, I'm not the least bit like you, really. Actually, I'm not brave at all and at school . . .' I lowered my voice. 'A couple of boys call me the Shrimp.'

'They'd better not call you the Shrimp while I'm around,' Brave Bill cried, 'or I'll have them walking the plank.'

When we reached Reema's house, I said, 'Brave Bill, you stand here, where she can't see you. Then you'll be a great surprise for her.' So Brave Bill waited at the top of her road.

I rang Reema's doorbell. She answered the door, dressed as Bart Simpson. She'd even covered her face in yellow powder.

'You look really good.'

'So do you.' Then she smiled sadly. 'So your magic cape didn't work last night?'

'Oh yes it did,' I said. 'But my brother

overheard us and sneaked in first. He's on
Brave Bill's pirate ship right now.'

'What a rotten trick!' Reema cried.

'But I've got a surprise for you.'

'For me?'

'Yeah, there's someone waiting for you
at the top of the road.'

She gave me a funny look. 'Who?'

'Go and see for yourself.'

Reema dashed out of her house, then let out a gasp of amazement as Brave Bill bowed to her.

'It can't be.'

'Oh yes it is,' he said. 'The one and only.'

'But this is just incredible,' she cried. 'I've never met a real-life, made-up person before.' She pulled out her little notebook. 'Can I have your autograph, please?'

Brave Bill signed his name in big bold letters in Reema's book.

'Thanks, I'll treasure this,' she cried.

'Treasure.' Brave Bill's eye opened wide. 'Oh, I see what you mean.'

On the way to school Reema and I kept sneaking glances at Brave Bill. We just couldn't believe he was walking to school with us.

We were walking through the gates when Elliot and Russell sprang out at us. They think they're tough. Today they were both dressed as characters from *Thunderbirds*.

'Look at the Shrimp,' Elliot shouted.

'He doesn't look anything like Brave Bill,' Russell sneered.

'Oh yes he does,' Reema cried. 'And you'd better be nice to Jamie because today he's got –'

'Reema,' I hissed. I'd told her we must keep Brave Bill's true identity a secret.

'Sorry,' she whispered back.

'Why should we be careful?' Russell demanded. 'What's the Shrimp going to do?'

He and Elliot started to laugh. Then Elliot pointed at Brave Bill. 'And who's that?'

'This is my friend, William, from far away, who's come to visit me,' I replied.

'Ahoy there, landlubbers,' Brave Bill said.

'I suppose you think that's funny,' Elliot snarled. 'You don't look anything like him anyway.'

Brave Bill started to go bright red.

'And the Brave Bill story is really stupid,' shouted Russell.

'Total rubbish,' agreed Elliot.

'One more word,' hissed Brave Bill, 'and I'll chop you both up and eat you with chips.'

'Oh yeah,' cried Elliot. But he didn't say anything else because Brave Bill was glaring at him so furiously.

Russell didn't say another word either. Well, not until he was some distance from us. Then he called out, 'I think it's stupid,

you both coming as the same person.
And why couldn't you come as someone
decent?'

I saw Brave Bill's hand start to twitch.
In another moment he'd have torn off his
eyepatch. 'Just ignore them,' I said.
'Please.'

'No one speaks like that to me,' Brave
Bill declared.

'They speak like that to Jamie every
day,' Reema said. 'And he never stands up
for himself.'

'Why not?' Brave Bill wanted to know,
staring right at me.

I hung my head. 'I told you why. I'm
nothing like you. Now just forget it and
come and meet our teacher, Mrs Davis.'

Mrs Davis was already in the
classroom, cleaning the board. 'Don't you
three look splendid,' she cried.

I introduced her to William.

'Pleased to meet you, William,' she said.

'At your service, ma'am,' Brave Bill replied, bowing very low.

Mrs Davis seemed a bit surprised by that. Then she asked Brave Bill where he lived.

'My home is the seven seas, ma'am,' he replied. 'I sail them all year, except for the weeks when I am on my own secret island, of course.'

By now Mrs Davis was looking totally astonished. But then Reema explained, 'He's pretending he's Brave Bill, the magic pirate.'

'So I see,' she murmured. 'Well, I haven't read the *Brave Bill* book myself.' Then she glanced down at Brave Bill's hands and saw all his rings. 'My goodness!' she exclaimed.

Brave Bill grinned. 'It saves me carrying money.'

'Well, we don't normally allow pupils to wear jewellery,' Mrs Davis said. 'But I don't suppose they're valuable.'

'Not valuable,' Brave Bill cried furiously. Then he muttered to me, 'Your teacher's a fool.'

Luckily, the rest of the class began streaming in. And a number did come over and say how good our costumes were. They especially admired Brave Bill's hat.

Brave Bill sat between Reema and me, staring around him as if fascinated by what he saw.

That morning Mrs Davis told us to write a story about the character we were pretending to be. But there was to be no talking when we were writing. And when Mrs Davis says 'no talking', she means it.

Soon everyone was working in silence – except for Brave Bill.

First of all he didn't have a pen.

'It's all right, I've got a spare one,' I whispered.

But after a few minutes he looked across at me. 'Can we swap? Your pen's blue and blue's my favourite colour.'

'Yeah, sure.'

While we swapped pens Mrs Davis clicked her tongue with exasperation.

A few more minutes went by and Brave Bill still hadn't written a single word. Reema and I tried to help.

'You must have had lots of adventures,' Reema said.

'So I have,' Brave Bill replied. 'And I write them all up in the ship's log at night. I sit on the deck staring up at all those millions of stars.' His eye was as bright as a star now. 'And I hear the waves lapping . . .'

'Everyone is being very good,' Mrs Davis said suddenly, 'and doing their work and concentrating, except for our visitor.' She stared at Brave Bill.

He glared back at her. Then he whispered to me, 'Can we set sail now?'

Reema giggled and I replied, 'We've got to stay here until ten past three.'

'But I'm bored already,' Brave Bill cried.

Mrs Davis put down the papers she was studying. 'William, are you still talking?'

'Yes, I am,' he replied cheerfully.

'Well, you're disturbing the whole class,' she said. 'You wouldn't behave like this at your school, would you?'

'I don't go to school any more, ma'am,' he replied. 'I left when I was eight.'

'I think you're being rather silly now,' replied Mrs Davis.

She called Brave Bill silly! His face was bright red and he was hissing really loudly. He sounded like a kettle about to boil.

And then he pulled off his eyepatch.

6. The Incredible Shrinking Teacher

Underneath the eyepatch was an eye sizzling with rage. You've never seen such an angry eye. It twitched and rolled furiously.

And then one of those sparks of anger shot right out of

Brave Bill's eye. It was just like a tiny speck of very bright light. And no one noticed it spring out of his eye except Reema and me.

She gasped and I cried, 'No, Brave Bill.' But we were too late. The spark set off like an arrow towards Mrs Davis.

One moment Mrs Davis was sitting at her desk as usual. The next, her head was

just peeping over the top of it. She looked down at her chair. Her feet didn't even reach the ground now. Then she swung herself off the chair, gazed around and gave a squeal of horror. And I didn't blame her at all. It must have been a really nasty shock for her, shrinking like that.

Her clothes had shrunk as well, so they all still fitted her. Which was one good thing, I suppose.

The other good thing was, she might have been smaller still. In fact, Brave Bill was about to shorten her even more, but I stopped him by hissing, 'No, don't, please.'

He frowned. His face was still scorching red but no more sparks flew out of his eye.

Mrs Davis tottered around her desk.

She could nearly walk under it now. Then she faced the class. 'Get on with your work,' she squeaked. Even her voice had shrunk. Now she was looking very alarmed indeed.

Meanwhile, all the pupils were just staring at her. Their mouths had dropped open in astonishment. And their eyes were popping out of their sockets. But no one, not even Russell or Elliot, said a word. They were too shocked.

Then the head teacher swept in. He always walked very quickly. In fact, his walking was like most people's running. He spoke very quickly, too. 'Ah, Mrs Davis, are these forms all completed? I do need them urgently.'

'Yes, they are,' Mrs Davis squeaked.

'Excellent, excellent, and I would like . . .' His voice trailed away, and for the first time he looked at Mrs Davis. He gazed down and down at her. Normally she was as tall as he was, but now she only came up to his stomach.

He jumped back from her in alarm. He removed his glasses and gave them a good clean. After this, he squinted down at her again. 'You seem somewhat shorter today, Mrs Davis.'

'Yes,' she squealed.

'Are you quite all right?'

'I'm not sure,' she quavered.

'No, well, I'd better get someone.' He walked, even more quickly than usual, to the door. 'Don't worry now.'

Then he was gone.

All at once Elliot began to laugh and then Russell called out, 'Miss, did you know you're shrinking?'

'Yes, yes, I had noticed,' she replied in her tiny little voice.

'Are you going to get any smaller?' Russell asked.

'I hope not.' She gazed about her anxiously.

'The incredible shrinking teacher,' Russell yelled.

And then Russell and Elliot both jumped on to their desks and started singing and dancing.

'Come down, come down at once.' Mrs Davis was trying to shout, but she couldn't.

'Sorry, can't hear you,' Russell cried.

Then they laughed and jeered at her. Russell even started eating a packet of crisps. (And Mrs Davis normally goes mad if you eat even a crumb in her class.)

This was awful.

I turned to Brave Bill. 'You can't leave Mrs Davis like that.'

'Why not?' he replied.

'Well, for a start, she'll never be able to teach again,' Reema cried.

'She shouldn't have called me silly, should she?' Brave Bill said huffily.

'Oh, please change her back,' Reema and I begged together.

Brave Bill frowned. 'All right. But if she annoys me again, well – I'll turn her into a maggot next time.'

He stared at Mrs Davis. She was jumping about anxiously, as the noise in her classroom grew louder.

Reema and I waited impatiently for Mrs Davis to start getting taller again.

But nothing happened.

Brave Bill scowled. 'I'm still angry. That's what it is. I can only make people grow back when I'm not cross with them.'

'Try and think of something happy then,' Reema suggested. 'Like when you're on your ship at night, looking up at all the stars.'

'Good idea,' said Brave Bill.

Immediately a large smile crossed his face. And at once Mrs Davis sprouted back up to her normal height.

The class gasped, while Mrs Davis looked dazed and confused.

'Will she be all right?' Reema wanted to know.

'Of course she will. She may feel a bit dizzy for a while, but that's all. And she won't remember anything that's just happened either.'

Mrs Davis gazed around at the class. Then she spotted Russell and Elliot jumping about on their desks, munching crisps.

'Whatever are you doing up there?' she snapped. 'And how dare you eat in my lesson. Get down at once.'

'Yes, miss,' they both said meekly. 'Sorry, miss.'

Mrs Davis shook her head at them. Then she sat down, blinking her eyes as if she'd just got off a merry-go-round that had been going too fast.

Suddenly we heard quick footsteps approaching. The head teacher bounced in again. And this time he'd brought someone with him.

'Ah, Mr Catton,' exclaimed Mrs Davis. 'I expect you've come for the forms.' And she handed him a stack of forms.

'Yes, thank you,' he replied. He turned to the person he'd brought with him. Our school nurse. Then he looked at Mrs Davis again.

'Er, Mrs Davis, would you mind standing up for a moment, please?'

'Standing up. Well, yes, all right,' Mrs Davis murmured, looking more than a little puzzled. She got to her feet and stared back at him. She was the same height as him again.

He staggered back. 'But you're . . .'

'Yes, Mr Catton?'

Both the school nurse and Mrs Davis were looking questioningly at him now.

'You're . . .' he said again. Then he muttered, 'I'm working too hard, that's what it is. I need a holiday,' and he rushed out of the door with the school nurse close behind him.

Brave Bill grinned. 'Now, that bit of the lesson I did enjoy.'

All the class were staring at Brave Bill and whispering, 'He must be the real one. He must.'

Suddenly Brave Bill called out, 'All right, ma'am, if I go and explore for a little bit?'

Mrs Davis, who was still looking a little confused, murmured, 'Yes, I suppose so.'

Brave Bill winked at Reema and me. 'See you later, landlubbers.' Then he bounced off.

Reema whispered, 'I'm glad he turned Mrs Davis back.'

'So am I.'

'He's got quite a bad temper, hasn't he?'

'I suppose so,' I agreed. 'He's still brilliant though, isn't he?'

'Oh yes,' she said quickly.

'But it's more trouble than I thought, taking a magic pirate into school. I wonder what's he's doing now?'

The minutes ticked by and Brave Bill still hadn't come back. Our school was quite small. He must have explored it all by now. So where was he?

Maybe the magic had worn off and he'd just disappeared.

That would be awful.

'Excuse me, Mrs Davis,' I called. 'May I go and check my friend William's all right – and hasn't got lost.'

She looked up. 'Well, be very quick now.'

I raced out of the classroom.

7. Thief in the School

Usually, when you're away from a lesson, the caretaker springs out at you, yelling fiercely, 'And what are you doing?' Then he pushes his head very close to yours. And you can even smell his breath. (It always smells of coffee.)

His name is Mr Tyrell. But we call him Mr Terror, because he's always cross and in a bad mood.

But today he was nowhere to be seen. And neither was Brave Bill.

I walked up and down the empty corridors. 'Brave Bill,' I hissed, 'are you hiding? You haven't gone, have you?'

And then, through the glass, I spotted him on the back field. I ran out.

He saw me and waved. 'Ahoy there.'

'I was getting worried,' I said. 'I thought the magic might have worn out.'

'Oh no. I've just been having a good look around.' But there was a strange expression on his face and I sensed he had been up to something.

We went back to the classroom.

Every five minutes Brave Bill would hiss in my ear, 'Is it time to eat our rations yet?'

And when morning lessons finally ended he was off like a hare to the dining hall. Reema and I have a packed lunch, so we sat at the packed-lunch table with Brave Bill. Aunt Nora had put in some extra jam sandwiches and fruit and chocolate for Brave Bill, all of which he wolfed down. Then he started looking longingly at the contents of Reema's lunch box. So of course she shared some of her food with him too.

All around us there was a lot of whispering about Brave Bill and his magic eye. But no one came up to us. I think they were all too scared.

A boy called Adam walked past our table. He's younger than Reema and me, but he usually eats his packed lunch with us. Today he looked very upset.

'What's wrong?' Reema asked.

'My mobile phone,' he exclaimed. 'At break time it was in my locker, but now it's vanished.'

'We'll help you look for it,' I said.

Reema and I searched all round the school. But Adam was right. It had vanished. It was a really good one too, all in silver.

And Adam's mobile phone wasn't the only thing to disappear out of the lockers. A girl's gold chain had gone. And some people's keys had gone missing too.

Soon everyone was looking for Mr Terror. Surely he must have seen who the thief was, he was always patrolling the corridors. But no one could find him either.

'Maybe Mr Terror has stolen all those things and run away with them,' Reema said.

She was joking, of course. But somebody must have robbed all those lockers. Then I had a really horrible thought: it wasn't Brave Bill, was it? He had been roaming about by himself for a long time. No, he would never do that, would he?

A crowd of pupils gathered round Reema, Brave Bill and me in the playground. There was a lot of murmuring and people kept giving Brave Bill suspicious glances. Then someone yelled, 'Brave Bill is a thief.'

Immediately he whirled around. 'Say that again and I'll make you walk the plank.'

At once everyone shrank back. It was Russell who'd called out. But he was too scared to own up. I watched him edging towards the back.

I turned to Brave Bill. I was very keen to defend his good name. 'Just tell everyone that you didn't take their belongings.'

'I can't do that.'

'Why not?'

Smirking now, Brave Bill replied, 'Because I did take them.'

There were gasps all around me. And I had this nasty, sinking feeling in my stomach.

'You didn't really,' Reema cried.

'Yes I did,' he said. 'I've got every one of those things.'

'But why?' I asked.

'Because I'm a pirate, and that's what pirates do. All those gold and shiny things belong to me now. It's my booty.'

A few people hissed him, but very quietly. Adam looked as if he was about to burst into tears. So did the girl whose gold chain had been stolen.

'Oh Brave Bill, you can't take their stuff. That's not fair,' I said. 'Give it back.'

Brave Bill gave me a furious glare. 'Be silent, you miserable slug.' Then he tapped his eyepatch. 'Or else.'

Reema whispered, 'Don't say any more, Jamie.'

And I could see Brave Bill becoming angrier and angrier. But I was furious too. I felt he had really let me down.

I was very scared too. In fact, I was petrified. But I swallowed down my fear, gulped twice and said, 'Brave Bill, you must give everyone back their things.'

'What did you say?' His face was the colour of a beetroot now.

A breathless silence fell on everyone.

'No one should steal other people's belongings, not even you,' I said in a shaky voice. 'And I'm telling you to give them back now.'

'I take orders from no one,' Brave Bill snapped. And then his hand swung up to his eyepatch.

Everyone, except Reema, stepped back two paces.

I stood there, trembling all over.

Any moment now I was about to start shrinking.

8. Treasure Map

I closed my eyes and waited for the worst to happen. I was pretty small already but in a moment I'd be half my normal size. Or maybe less than that. Someone let out a yell. I shut my eyes even tighter.

Then I heard a voice call my name. It sounded just like Reema. I opened my eyes. It *was* Reema. And she was smiling at me. There was no sign of Brave Bill either.

'He just walked off,' she whispered.
I let out a great sigh of relief.
'And he threw this piece of paper on to
the ground,' Reema

went on. 'It's got
your name on it.'

I unfolded the paper. At the top of the page was a picture of a skull and crossbones and two words:

TREASURE MAP

The map showed the back field. Now, behind this field is a wood. We weren't supposed to go into this wood, not ever. And there was a large wire fence separating our field from it. But there was

a gap in the fence. And Brave Bill had
marked this gap on the map. After which
he'd written in huge letters:

'TO FIND THE TREASURE: WALK
SEVEN PACES THEN TURN TWO PACES
TO YOUR RIGHT.'

'This might be a trap,' Reema said.

'Maybe, but I'll have to go and see.'

'If any teachers catch you in the wood, they'll go mad,' she warned.

'I'll be all right.'

'You will if I act as lookout,' she replied.

We rushed off. A few people from my class, including Russell and Elliot, followed us. But no one got too close. I think they were afraid Brave Bill was lurking near by.

The gap in the fence was pretty small. But then, so am I. So I scrambled through it easily enough. After which I counted out seven paces, then took two more paces to the right and looked up. A massive oak tree loomed in front of me. At the bottom of the tree was a mound of sticks and leaves. This must be where Brave Bill had buried his booty.

I crouched down and started digging under the leaves with my ruler.

'Stay still,' Reema hissed. 'Mrs Davis is coming.'

I froze – and waited.

'It's all right,' whispered Reema a few moments later. 'She's gone again. She was looking for Mr Terror. Have you found anything yet?'

'Not yet.' I carried on digging. Then I cried, 'Result!'

'What have you found?' Reema asked.

'One gold chain.' Then I dug up Adam's mobile phone. Soon I'd retrieved all the stolen goods.

Reema and I carried them proudly back to school. Adam was so pleased to have the mobile phone back he slapped me on the back, while the girl whose gold chain had been stolen gave me a kiss.

'There was no need to do that,' Reema sniffed.

Russell and Elliot stood watching all this. Then Russell said to me, 'You did pretty well. Even though it was your fault all those things got stolen.'

'It wasn't Jamie's fault,' Reema said at once.

'Yes it was,' Russell argued. 'After all, if the Shrimp hadn't brought Brave Bill into school, none of this would have happened. Still, well done, Shrimp.'

'And stop calling me the Shrimp.' I said this so loudly Russell and Elliot jumped back from me. 'I don't like it.'

'No, fair enough,' Elliot said. 'See you then, Jamie.' And he and Russell ran off.

'I'd like to say "well done" too,' Reema said. 'The way you stood up to Brave Bill like that, I was very proud of you.'

I hoped I wasn't turning bright red. 'But inside I was very scared,' I admitted.

'That just makes you even braver. After all, you didn't have a magic eye to help you, did you?' Then she added, 'I don't like Brave Bill any more.'

'Why not?'

'I think he's a bit creepy. And I wish I hadn't given him three of my sandwiches.'

Suddenly a thought struck me. 'Don't you think it's a bit strange no one's seen Mr Terror all lunchtime? Hadn't we better go to his office and check Brave Bill didn't . . . Well, shall we just see?'

We knocked nervously on the door of Mr Terror's office.

'There's no answer,' Reema whispered.

I opened the door slowly. 'Mr Tyrell,' I called. Then I thought I heard something. 'Listen.'

'I can't hear anything,' Reema murmured.

But I did – a tiny, squeaking sound. 'I think Mr Terror is here. Only very much smaller than usual.'

'Oh no,' Reema gasped. 'Well, we must find him.'

We searched around Mr Terror's office. There was a table and a chair in there, a noticeboard with a rota in big letters at the top, and a line of hooks with keys on them. There was also a large cupboard which was locked. And in the corner was a sink.

Suddenly, Reema let out a cry. 'Look.' In the sink was a jam jar. And inside the jam jar was Mr Terror. He was banging against the glass and looking very angry. He was trying to speak too. But all he could do was give off these high-pitched squeaks.

It was so weird to see Mr Terror, no bigger than my finger now, but still wearing his brown overall.

'It's good how, when people shrink, their clothes shrink too, isn't it?' I whispered to Reema.

She nodded, then added, 'I don't think

Mr Terror is too impressed though.'

And he went on banging against the glass.

I put my face down to the jar. 'Just relax, Mr Tyrell. We'll have you back to your normal size soon.'

'Will we?' Reema asked.

'I don't know. I was only trying to cheer him up. I wonder where Brave Bill's gone.'

At that moment the door creaked open, and there was Brave Bill. He saw Mr Terror in the jam jar and laughed.

'Why did you put Mr Terror in there?' Reema demanded.

'Because he's a right misery-bucket,' Brave Bill replied. 'And he made me angry.'

'Everyone makes you angry,' Reema murmured.

'Will you turn him back?' I asked Brave Bill.

'I suppose so,' he said reluctantly. 'Tip him out of the jam jar.'

I unscrewed the lid and carefully shook Mr Terror on to my fairly clean handkerchief.

'Stroke his head,' Reema suggested. 'He's probably feeling a bit scared.'

I moved my hand near him. Mr Terror promptly shook a tiny fist up at me.

'He's not very friendly, is he?' Reema muttered.

'Put him on the ground and I'll turn him back,' Brave Bill said.

So I lowered Mr Terror down on to my handkerchief, then hissed, 'Cheer up, won't be long now.'

Mr Terror raised two tiny fists at me this time.

But then, in the blink of an eye, he grew back to my size. And in another blink, he was his usual height again.

He scowled at the three of us. 'What are you all doing in my office? I never said you could come in here.'

I couldn't think what to say. 'Well, er, Mr Terror . . .'

'How dare you call me that! My name is Mr Tyrell, as you very well know.' And both his chins wobbled furiously.

'I'm very sorry,' I began.

'And who dropped this dirty handkerchief?' he demanded.

'Er, I think that's mine, actually,' I said.

He hurled it at me, and the three of us made a hasty exit.

'He wasn't at all grateful to us for turning him back,' said Reema.

'We should have left him in the jam

jar,' said Brave Bill. 'Anyway, I'm going now. I've had enough of school.'

'Bye then,' Reema called. 'Hope I never see you again,' she added, under her breath.

'See you, Brave Bill,' I said. But he was already walking away. I stared after him.

Reema gave my arm a squeeze. 'Come on, let's forget him.'

When I walked into the classroom all the pupils clapped and cheered me, as if I were a famous footballer. They went on clapping. Just about everyone knew how I'd stood up to Brave Bill.

But I felt really flat and let down. Brave Bill was my all-time favourite character. And we'd got on so well at first. But we'd parted on very bad terms. And I'd probably never see him again.

During the afternoon someone said

they'd seen Brave Bill hanging around outside. I rushed to the window but I couldn't spot him.

I walked home with Reema as usual. She tried to cheer me up and said she'd pop round later.

I rang the doorbell. Aunt Nora opened the door and smiled at me. She seemed especially happy this afternoon. I wondered if Harry had come back. No doubt he'd have lots of tales about his day as a pirate.

I followed Aunt Nora into the kitchen. And there, sitting at the table, eating yet another enormous meal, was Brave Bill.

9. Message in a Milk Bottle

Brave Bill had taken his hat off and was really tucking into the meal Aunt Nora had prepared.

'He said he was still hungry,' Aunt Nora explained.

Beside him was a huge pile of sandwiches. 'My shipmates are going to love these,' he said, nodding at them.

'I made forty-three. So no one's left

out,' Aunt Nora said.

Brave Bill gave a happy sigh. 'A delicious meal, ma'am. Thanks again.' Then he looked at me. 'I suppose I'd better get back to my story.'

'Oh, must you go?' Aunt Nora cried.

'The sea's calling me back,' Brave Bill replied.

'Well, have a safe journey,' Aunt Nora said. 'And I hope we see you again.'

'Yes, I'd like to drop anchor here again one day,' Brave Bill said.

He and I walked up the stairs in

silence. I was still cross with him, yet I didn't want him to go either. I was all mixed up and didn't know what to say.

I went to the bathroom, splashed water on the cape and brought it back to my bedroom. Brave Bill was standing there, the box of sandwiches under his arm.

Still neither of us spoke.

Then I mumbled to the cape, 'Number Seven, please take Brave Bill back to his story.'

I looked up at him. 'The magic's a bit creaky, so you might have to wait a few minutes.'

To my surprise Brave Bill smiled right at me.

'So where did you go after you left Reema and me?' I asked.

'Oh, I hung around at your school for a while,' he replied.

'Someone said they saw you.'

'Well, there was something I wanted to see.'

'What was that?' I asked.

'You being cheered when you walked into your classroom. It made me very happy to see that.' And his eyes suddenly lit up.

Now I was confused. 'Why did that make you happy?'

'Because you're much braver than you thought. But it took Brave Bill to show you, didn't it?' He was grinning from ear to ear now.

'What do you mean . . .' I began.

Then in a flash I realized the truth.

'All those things you took – you didn't really want any of them, did you?' I cried.

'Of course I didn't. We've got a secret

island full of treasure.'

'You took those things so I'd have to stand up to you.'

'Well, I hoped you would, yes. But you did even better than I'd hoped. I especially liked the way you said to me, "I'm telling you to give them back now." You showed real courage today, Jamie.' Then he started to float up into the air. 'Ah, looks like I'm off at last. Well, all the best, shipmate.'

Shipmate. He'd never called me that before. I glowed with pride. 'Thanks for everything, Brave Bill. I wish you could stay longer. I'll miss you.'

Brave Bill laughed and said something else, just as he whirled away through the ceiling. I only caught the last word, which I think was 'bottle'. And then he was gone. My bedroom seemed very quiet and empty without him.

I sank down on my bed. Then I saw another figure drifting down through the ceiling.

It was Harry.

He waved at me. And when he reached the ground he bounded over to me and gave me a big hug.

'Stop trying to get round me. I'm very cross with you,' I said.

He gave me his hurt look. 'But I'm just pleased to see you, and glad to be home.'

'Didn't you enjoy being a pirate then?'

He shook his head.

'Why ever not?'

'Because . . .' his voice fell away to a whisper. 'Because I was seasick nearly the whole time and spent most of the day being sick over the side of the ship.'

I started to smile.

'And they gave me this gruel which they said would make me feel better. But, ugh, it was really disgusting – and it just made me feel even worse.'

I was laughing out loud now.

'It's not funny,' Harry cried.

'Yes it is. It's very, very funny.'

Harry sat down on my bed and yawned. 'And I hardly saw Brave Bill. He was away somewhere.'

'Yes, he was here with me.'

Harry's eyes opened wide. 'What?' But then he yawned again. 'Oh, I'm too tired to talk now. I couldn't sleep on my hammock, so I'm going to have a little nap on your bed. Do you mind?'

'No, I don't mind.'

'Thanks, Jamie. I really missed you. I should have wished for you to come with me.'

He curled up on my bed, and a few seconds later he was fast asleep.

I sat on the chair in the corner of my room, thinking about my incredible day. Then I picked up the *Brave Bill* book. Harry had already vanished from the last page and Brave Bill was back there again, but now looking a little plumper than he had before. It must have been all the food he'd eaten today.

Harry stirred and stretched. 'Hello, Jamie. I've just had the weirdest dream. I dreamt your cape was magic and I wished myself on to a ship with Brave Bill, only I kept getting seasick.'

I gaped at him.

Then Aunt Nora came in. 'Oh, there you are, Harry. Did you have a good day at school?'

'I think so,' Harry replied. 'I can't

remember much about it now.'

She laughed. 'Well, would you pop
down to the shops for me, dear? I've run
out of bread. I was sure I had two fresh
loaves but I can't find them anywhere.'

I listened to Harry and Aunt Nora with
growing astonishment. Now the wish was

over, they'd both forgotten everything that had happened.

The doorbell rang.

It was Reema. She burst in and hissed at me, 'Jamie, you don't suppose Brave Bill took all those things deliberately. Then you'd have to stand up to him and you'd realize . . .'

'That's exactly why he did take them,' I interrupted her. 'He explained it all to me.'

'He's very clever, isn't he? I always liked him and I'm glad he ate three of my sandwiches. Is he still here?'

'No, he left ages ago. And he's back in his story again.'

Her face fell. 'What a shame. I wanted to say a proper goodbye to him. Still, at least I've got his autograph.'

'Do you know the really weird thing?' I

said. 'Neither Aunt Nora nor Harry remembers anything that's happened today.'

'I bet our class won't either,' Reema murmured. 'But that's the way the cape's magic works. No one remembers what's happened except you.' She paused for a moment. 'And me, for some reason.'

'I expect that's because you're my very special friend,' I said.

She nodded and smiled.

'So Elliot and Russell will be back calling me "the Shrimp" again tomorrow.'

'No they won't,' Reema replied, 'because you'll stand up for yourself now.'

I grinned. 'That's right, I will.'

Aunt Nora popped her head round the door. 'Hello, Reema dear.' Then she turned to me. 'I was just putting the milk bottles out when I found something in one of them. A funny-looking note, addressed to you.'

I grabbed it from Aunt Nora.

'One of your little games, I expect,' smiled Aunt Nora, before disappearing back into the kitchen.

I stared at Reema excitedly. 'Just before he zoomed off, Brave Bill was trying to tell me something. I only caught the last word – "bottle".'

'He was saying he'd left you a message in the milk bottle,' Reema said, getting excited too. 'Well, open it, for goodness' sake.'

The paper was brown and old-looking and it was burnt round the edges. It looked like a scroll. I unfurled it and read the message. Then I read the message again.

Reema was jumping about beside me.

'What does it say?' she demanded.

'It's a bit peculiar, really.'

She snatched it from me and read aloud: 'Look under your bed. Brave Bill.'

'What on earth do you suppose that means?' I cried.

'At a guess, I'd say go and look under your bed,' Reema snapped. 'Come on, Jamie, what are you waiting for?'

'Nothing. It's just not what I was expecting.'

'Well, I'm going to look under your bed anyhow,' Reema cried.

She bolted up the stairs. I raced after her and overtook her outside my bedroom. Then I crouched down, gazed under my bed, and exclaimed, 'I don't believe it!'

'Don't believe what?' Reema cried, trying to see over my shoulder.

'Look at this.' And from under the bed I brought out Brave Bill's hat.

Her eyes gleamed. 'Oh, wow.'

'I know. It's incredible. He's left his totally brilliant pirate hat behind for me.'

'He must have liked you a lot.'

'It's incredible,' I said again. I didn't know what else to say, I was just so shocked and thrilled.

'Well, try it on then,' Reema urged.

Very carefully I put Brave Bill's hat on my head. 'What do you think? Do I look like Brave Bill now?'

Reema shook her head. 'No, you look exactly like Brave Jamie.'